Big Rig

Grader Kat

Monster Truck Max

Pumper Pat

Hook and Ladder Lucy

Izzy Ice Cream Truck

Ice Cream

Tow Truck Ted

To trucktastic Jeff Norton

—J. S.

SIMON & SCHUSTER BOOKS FOR YOUNG READERS
An imprint of Simon & Schuster Children's Publishing Division
1230 Avenue of the Americas, New York, New York 10020
Copyright © 2014 by JRS Worldwide, LLC
TRUCKTOWN and JON SCIESZKA'S TRUCKTOWN and design are trademarks of JRS Worldwide, LLC.
All rights reserved, including the right of reproduction in whole or in part in any form.
SIMON & SCHUSTER BOOKS FOR YOUNG READERS is a trademark of Simon & Schuster, Inc.
For information about special discounts for bulk purchases, please contact
Simon & Schuster Special Sales at 1-866-506-1949 or business@simonandschuster.com.
The Simon & Schuster Speakers Bureau can bring authors to your live event.
For more information or to book an event, contact the Simon & Schuster Speakers Bureau
at 1-866-248-3049 or visit our website at www.simonspeakers.com.
Book design by Laurent Linn
The text for this book is set in Truck King.
The illustrations for this book are rendered digitally.
Manufactured in China
0714 SCP
2 4 6 8 10 9 7 5 3 1
Library of Congress Cataloging-in-Publication Data
Scieszka, Jon.
Race from A to Z / written by Jon Scieszka ; characters and environments developed
by the Design Garage, David Gordon, Loren Long, David Shannon. — First edition.
pages cm. — (Jon Scieszka's Trucktown)
Summary: Dump trucks, fire trucks, and even garbage trucks join in a race
through the streets of Trucktown.
ISBN 978-1-4169-4136-1 (hardback) — ISBN 978-1-4424-5321-0 (eBook)
[1. Stories in rhyme. 2. Racing—Fiction. 3. Trucks—Fiction. 4. Alphabet—Juvenile fiction.]
I. Design Garage. II. Title.
PZ8.3.S347Jon 2014
[E]—dc23
2012046633

first
edition

Characters and environments
developed by the

DAVID SHANNON
LOREN LONG
DAVID GORDON

Illustrated by

DANI JONES

RACE
from A to Z

Written by JON SCIESZKA

SIMON & SCHUSTER BOOKS FOR YOUNG READERS

New York London Toronto Sydney New Delhi

A is for **A**xle. **B**umper starts with **B**.

Jack shouts out to Trucktown, "Let's all race to **Z**!"

"Calling all trucks—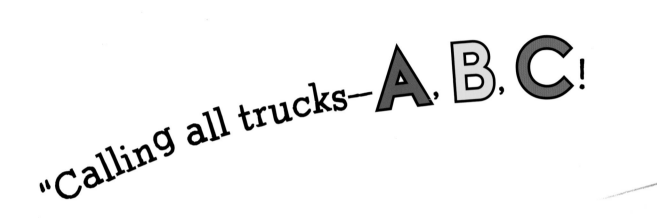A, B, C!

Let's go, trucks—race from A to Z!"

C is for Construction,
Curbs and Cones and Crashes!

D is for Dan Dump Truck, who Dumps his Dirt then Dashes!

E is for Every Engine.

Vroom! Vroom! Vroom!

G is Gabby Garbage Truck,
collecting all our junk.

H-**H**er **H**orn **H**igh on **H**er **H**ead.

Hink!

Honk!

Hunk!

STOP

I is Izzy—

"Not while we are racing, Izzy!"

"Ice cream! Ice cream! Do you want an Ice cream?"

"Let's go, trucks—race from **A** to **Z**!"

J is Just for Jack Truck,
leader of the pack.

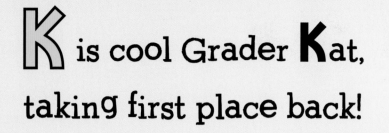

K is cool Grader **K**at,
taking first place back!

L is for Lucy Ladder truck.
Lucy Loves this trick.

M is **M**elvin **M**ixer.... *Yikes!*
Freaked out by a stick.

N is for **N**ine **N**ew lug **N**uts, keeping wheels on tight.

P is Plenty Potholes,

messing up the street.

Time to take a detour.
(Thanks, **P**ayloader **P**ete.)

Q often means "**Quiet**" in a different place.

In Trucktown Q means "Quite." QUITE LOUD! when we race.

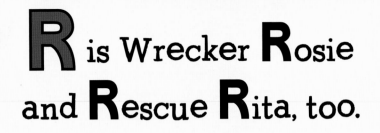

R is Wrecker **R**osie
and **R**escue **R**ita, too.

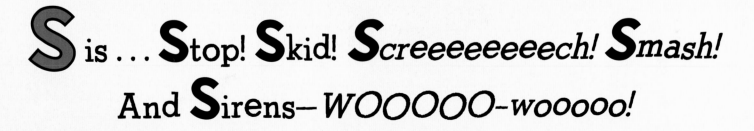

S is ... **S**top! **S**kid! **S**creeeeeeeech! **S**mash!
And **S**irens— *WOOOOO-wooooo!*

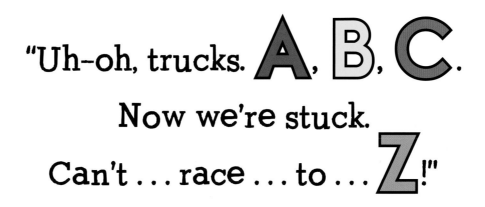

"Uh-oh, trucks. A, B, C.
Now we're stuck.
Can't ... race ... to ... Z!"

Hooray for **T**–**T**ed **T**ow **T**ruck.
Ted can save the day!

U–we are **U**ntangled.

VVVV**R**OOOM! Back on our way.

W is Whirling Wheels,

spinning to the end.

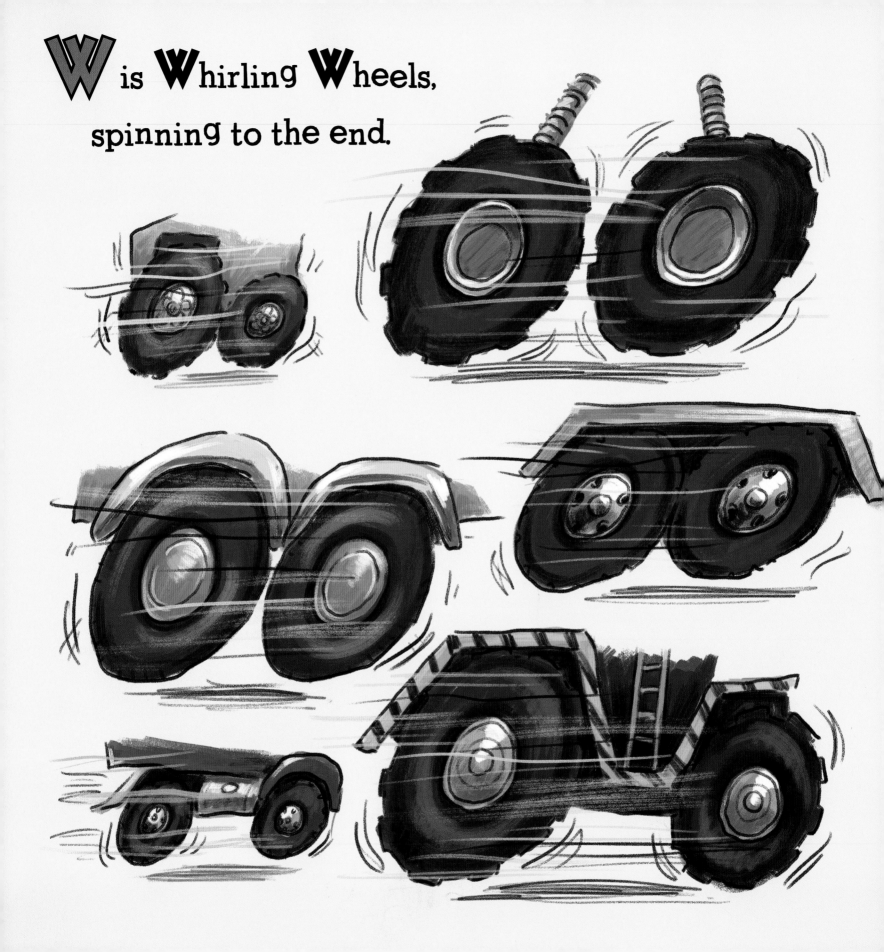

Yes! There is the finish line.

Just around that bend.

Look out—**X**! A **X**ylophone?
No one knows just why
scary Big Rig has one.

(You ask him, tough guy.)

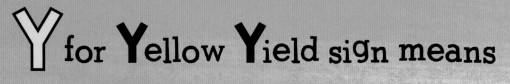

Y for **Y**ellow **Y**ield sign means slow, not stop or go.

YIELD

So, who will win the race?
Yell it if you know.

Gabriella Garbage Truck

MAY 2018
(2014)

Rescue Rita

Dump Truck Dan

Payloader Pete

Jack Truck

Wrecking Crane Rosie

Cement Mixer Melvin